THE DEMON SLAYERS

Laura Shenton

THE DEMON SLAYERS

Laura Shenton

Iridescent Toad Publishing

Iridescent Toad Publishing.

Cover by Mc Damon.

First edition. ISBN: 978-1-913779-44-3

*Extra special thanks to Des M. Astor
for helping me bring this book to life.*

The Demon Slayers

Chapter One

Many colours decorated the paper in front of her. The young woman gently traced a brush along the smooth surface, her own humming comforting her in the dull light of the room as the stars shone brightly outside. With her raven hair spilling down her back in silken waves, a soft smile played on her lips.

Deep in thought, she admired the misty blues and royal purples of her freshly-painted night scene. Moths danced with fireflies while tiny silver fox kits joyfully explored the terrain at the front of the painting. Owls peered out from behind the leaves of various trees, their eyes glowing with wonder rather than with any malicious intent. Dusty greys, cold blues, and midnight blacks brought the night scene to life, harmonising with the brighter colours of the stars and moon above.

Longingly, the woman turned her focus towards her bedroom window. Enjoying the cool breeze that rushed in, her mind turned to thoughts of going for a refreshing walk through the woods.

I'd love to go for a walk. I'd have to go past my family on the way out though. I really don't feel like dealing with…

"Raylene?" a gruff masculine voice sounded out from behind her bedroom door.

She tensed and groaned.

It looks like I'll have to face them tonight anyway.

A harsh knock on the door shattered any remaining focus that Ray may have had on the painting.

"Come in," she said with a sigh.

A tall, lithe man entered the room. A smart fellow, his black hair was slicked back and he wore a dark, refined suit with a pocket that held a red handkerchief. His pale skin was littered with laceration scars. As Ray looked up to meet her father's deep-crimson gaze, anxiety pooled in the pit of her stomach.

He stared back at her for a few moments before looking around to examine the room. It was gloomy, but comfortable. The walls were decorated with various art pieces, similar to what Ray had been working on prior to his interruption. His lips twisted into a scowl as he exhaled sharply, his voice taking on his usual tone of disappointment.

"You missed midnight training for this? Again?! Raylene?"

The venom dripping from his voice sent a shiver down Ray's spine. She ran her tongue over her feline-like fangs that had subconsciously started to extend – it always happened when she was upset, and this situation was no exception. Against the silence, she clenched her jaw and stared at the floor.

"Don't click your fangs at me, Raylene," her father chastised.

He took a few steps closer towards his daughter, an onslaught of harsh words about to begin. When she winced, he sighed.

"Rather than directing your anger at *me*, when I am genuinely trying to get you to see reason, why don't you have that same vigour when we are speaking about serious matters?" he asked, his voice softer than before, but still laced with agitation.

Swallowing hard, Ray closed her eyes, searching for the right words to say. The truth was, all she longed to do was paint, especially on this particular night after yet another exhausting argument with her mother. The subject had been the same as the previous night.

"I lost track of the time, Father," Ray replied, trying hard to hide her frustration. "Honestly, I had been planning on attending the training session. I just became so immersed in my painting."

Sounding unconvinced, her father scoffed and strolled over. He looked at the painting in front of her. A silence settled in before he spoke in a defeated tone.

"You have so much talent, Raylene. You paint beautiful scenes that capture the world around us. Unfortunately though, we cannot ever hope to enjoy it unless we purge the demons. They are a *danger* to us. Why you can't understand that, I do not know."

"I… understand," Ray replied.

She hung her head, unable to escape the overbearing feeling of guilt. The subject had been drilled into her over the years, but she had only ever pretended to pay attention. Something about the teachings seemed off to her, but she had never been overly vocal about it. It would have only caused more friction, especially in how her family were so certain of them.

"Do you really understand though?" her father asked. "You waste time on this hobby of yours when you should be training. You are a powerful woman, I have seen it."

Ray didn't know where to look as her father continued to chastise her, gesturing around the room at her art.

"If you *ever* want to be able to do all of *this* without fear, you will need to listen to me," he insisted.

Ray nodded. Although her father's tone was harsh, she believed that he was coming from a place of caring – mostly anyway. He didn't dismiss her like her mother did.

"I know," Ray muttered. "Demons are a danger to vampires. We need to destroy them if we are to have any hope of peace. I understand – even if no one around me knows *what* exactly started this mentality."

"It doesn't matter," her father said harshly.

Giving a low, guttural growl from the pit of his chest, he reached up and ran his claws through his hair, frustrated at Ray's lack of engagement. He couldn't grasp why she wasn't like the rest of the family – focused and merciless. Noticing that Ray was clenching her fist and staring at the art piece before her with malice, he once again softened.

"Just show up to training in a few hours," he said. "Promise me. I will leave you to this work of yours. It is stunning art, but it doesn't keep our family safe in the grand scheme of things."

"I will," Ray said shortly.

She clenched her jaw until her father had left the room and closed the door behind him. The frustration rushing through her veins struck deeply as she took one of the containers of paint and angrily threw it down at her work, causing crimson liquid to splatter everywhere, including upon herself. The mess was worse for the shards of hardened clay that flew out in many directions. Luckily, none of them sliced into her hands.

The paint stained her flesh, reminding her of blood. She stared at the splotches on the scene before her. It was no longer serene, and instead, a battlefield.

It looks terrible…

As it dawned on her that she'd ruined her work beyond repair, tears began to crawl down Ray's cheeks. Hours upon hours of effort had been destroyed in a moment of blind rage.

Not bothering to dab any of the red paint off, she despairingly decided to abandon the piece.

What's the point? It would just mix with the other colours and spoil them.

She made her way to her bathroom. Standing at the sink, she slowly turned the tap on, letting the water run until it had reached the perfect temperature. She grabbed the soap, working it into a generous lather as she mixed it with the water. As she began to wash her hands, she caught sight of herself in the mirror, her tired, blood-red gaze staring back at her.

"Why can't you be like them?" she asked herself. "You're supposed to be hungry for battle, for the good of the family. Demons are horrible – they're evil. They've always been an enemy of our kind."

She was still unsure. Although she had heard numerous tales of how awful and chaotic demons could be, she had never encountered one herself. Vampires and humans had long since moved on from their conflicts, mostly. In contrast, demons were said to be irredeemable.

Ray wandered back into her room and collapsed upon a soft armchair with onyx-toned cushioning. She gazed at the various art pieces that she had created before, all depicting parts of her world.

Lar was a dazzling place to behold. By night, the wings of the butterbats created mesmerising illuminations as the playful critters danced in flight across the midnight sky. The incredible lightshow beneath the moon and stars always filled Ray's heart with joy.

A sad smile played on her lips as she observed the other paintings she had done. Wide swathes of woodland served as home to creatures like the lypines – large fox-beasts that made their cousins look more like fox-mice than full vulpines! Despite their appearance, lypines were gentle giants; their thick, burly heads sometimes knocked against the tall trees when they got drunk on fermented fruit. Ray reminisced about the time she had fed one some boar meat from her hunt. That night, she felt she had made a friend. However, when she shared the experience with her family, they didn't approve.

The pleasant memory faded into nothing as Ray realised that she wasn't wandering the woods. She was in her room; miserable and wishing that she was somewhere else.

Perhaps when I finish training, I can go for a walk, or something.

Shrugging, she grumpily wandered over to a pristine wooden bookcase. Plucking a book from the shelf, she settled into her comfortable chair. Furthering her knowledge on the flora and fauna of Lar would not only inspire her next painting, but also serve as a welcome distraction.

Try as she might, she couldn't fully immerse herself in the book. Instead, she postponed going downstairs by cleaning up the shards of her shattered paint container. She tossed the mess into the bin, but left the ruined painting where it was. She couldn't bear to look at it.

Sighing heavily and mustering up the last of her willpower, she finally approached her door, bracing herself for the training her father had insisted upon.

Chapter Two

Ray wandered through the deep, dark halls of her family's large home, strolling past numerous rooms. In some of them, a vast array of books detailed the various wars her kind had participated in, the subject of demons naturally a heavy topic in most. Beyond that, the rooms held various things, such as furs from the beasts of Lar; the garments were there to provide warmth to the humans who served the house. There was also entertainment, such as board games and puzzles.

There was only one room with a locked door. Ray had never been in there before. Her family had made it clear that she must keep out. Although she had never questioned them on it, she couldn't deny her curiosity.

Shoving thoughts of the room to the back of her mind, she continued onwards. Some of the rooms contained fantasy books. With their portrayal of worlds outside of Lar that encouraged the imagination to run wild, every now and then, Ray would indulge, appreciating the opportunity to distract herself from the gloom of her reality. Even her father enjoyed a fantasy tale from time to time. Her mother, on the other hand, was far too stubborn to engage.

Ray gulped at the thought of having to face her mother.

As she descended the stairs, she passed paintings that displayed scenes of bloody battles. Her family was so obsessed with war, that the intricacy of the artwork was wasted on them. To Ray, the serene peace of the woods in the backgrounds was far more appealing than any grisly conflict.

The candlelight ahead of Ray alerted her to the family gathering. She was just in time for dinner, which she often missed when getting carried away with her art. Sometimes, rather than getting a snack, she would skip food entirely. To miss a meal wasn't good for a vampire like her; if she got too hungry, she could lose control and hurt someone – something that she had no desire to do. The loud rumble in her stomach reminded her of the fact that she should pay more attention to her needs.

A melodic feminine voice rang through the air, cutting into Ray's train of thought like a shard of glass as she entered the dining room.

"Raylene," said her mother. "How wonderful of you to join us, and clearly, you're hungry. Perhaps you should waste less time making rubbish, and instead, focus on your body's upkeep so that eventually, you can be useful in battle."

Fixing her gaze on the fancily-carved mahogany table, Ray held her tongue. After a pause, she looked up and met her mother's silver eyes. The older female vampire had her hair done up in a tight bun, with just a few strands falling onto her face. She wore tight leather for ease of movement, which showcased her toned musculature. In the event of a war, Ray and her mother were expected to take the lead in any battle. Ray's father and brother would provide support if necessary, but their main role was in taking care of the home. Despite their battle skills, the household operated under a strong matriarchal structure.

Both Ray and her mother had ghostly-pale skin. However, the older woman had deep scarring all over hers – mostly from demon bites, no less. Although Ray always performed well in training after many years of practice, she had never been in a real battle.

Putting her hands on her hips, Ray's mother glared at her in disapproval. She looked as though she had more to say, but sitting at the other side of the table, Ray's father cleared his throat.

"Now, Dear, Ray was just expressing her talents in other areas," he said patiently. "You know that I too would prefer her to focus on what matters, but calling her art rubbish is going a bit too far."

Ray's mother bared her fangs, her spiteful gaze falling upon her husband. He shrank back a little at this, breaking the stare and humbly knitting his fingers together. The scent of discomfort permeated the air, causing Ray's stomach to churn. She hated seeing her parents like this, and her mother caused it so frequently.

"I don't need commentary from you," the female vampire snapped at her husband. "You enable her, and you're far too easy on her. If I had my way, all of the *rubbish* up there would be obliterated. She wastes too much time on something so meaningless."

As she turned to look at Ray, the annoyance in the woman's tone only deepened. She decisively pointed a claw at her daughter.

"I want to see you giving it your all in training out there tonight. Do I make myself clear, Raylene?"

Ray nodded.

"Good. I am utterly sick of your passive attitude."

With that, Ray's mother stormed out of the room. Ray sat down on one of the wooden chairs at the table – next to her father and across from her brother, Alden. He was dressed in a simple, charcoal-coloured informal vest. He wore loose-fitting trousers of a slightly darker colour. As much as he had wanted to rip them into a custom style, in not wishing to face the wrath of his disapproving mother, he had thought better of it.

As usual, during their mother's outburst, Alden

had remained silent. Some of his shaggy black hair fell into his eyes as he gave his sister a look of sympathy. He was only a year older than her, and rarely spoke up against their mother. Perhaps it was better that way; he didn't want to say the wrong thing and prolong the older woman's ranting.

Ray's father grimaced, shaking his head.

"I'm glad you could make it to dinner, Ray," he said. "Your mother just wants the best for us. I don't think she truly believes what she says. She's just worried that the demons will gain ground and overrun us."

"You can try and convince me of lies all you like, Father, but I know the truth," Ray replied, agitated. "She's ashamed of me. I'll prove myself out there in training, but it will never be enough for her. We both know that she wants to force me into fighting a real battle."

Ray's father gave a resigned nod, fidgeting with the napkin before him and letting out a defeated sigh.

"Well," he said. "Let's eat."

He reached for the bell in the centre of the table, and gently rang it. A few seconds later, three human servants entered the room, their necks and wrists displaying many pinpricks. Their expressions were neutral and unbothered; this was business as usual to them.

One of them approached Ray. They gave a bow before bending forwards, and then tilted their head to expose their neck.

"Thank you for your service," Ray told the human.

Gently leaning down and running her tongue over the vein in the human's neck, Ray used her fangs to delicately pierce the skin. The warm silken liquid poured down her throat, revitalising her. The high quality of the blood was due to the excellent health of the servants. They were kept on a diet of game, which Ray's parents always hunted.

Upon finishing her meal, Ray drew her tongue over the human's wound, closing it with the chemicals in her saliva. Her fangs retracted, and she gave a smile as the human bowed, evidently at ease with the ritual.

Alden, meanwhile, had blood dripping down his chin. Unable to catch it with his tongue, he grabbed his napkin and dabbed at it quickly, his face flushing in embarrassment. Their father looked at him with disappointment and concern.

"You need to learn how to eat without making such a mess," he scolded.

Ray awkwardly played with her napkin for a moment before taking a sip from her glass of water.

Her father rang the bell again, prompting more human servants to enter the room. Imbued with the scents from the kitchen, they carried in trays of baked goods containing iced cupcakes and dark chocolate brownies. As delicious as the blood had been, Ray salivated at the thought of the sweet desserts. The vast majority of her diet was strictly blood from humans, but her kind still needed extra sugars for complete nourishment. She snatched up a brownie, and took an enthusiastic bite, enjoying the rich, sumptuous taste as it settled on her tongue. It was a welcome distraction from what she feared would be a tough night.

Little conversation occurred throughout the rest

of dinner. It was the norm in Ray's family. She wasn't in the mood to talk, and was still soured by just how rude her mother had been.

Despite her familiarity with the room, Ray turned her head to look around. She wanted to avoid engaging with anyone at the table. She admired the delicate porcelain dishes inside one of the glass cabinets; they sparkled beneath the subtle light of the crystal chandelier. The chairs, made from the same gracefully-carved wood as the table, rested upon a thick carpet woven with threads of crimson, black, and gold. Though she could appreciate the splendour of her environment, it often felt superficial, especially considering how often she felt unwelcome there.

Satisfied that she'd had a good meal, Ray gave a respectful nod before standing up and making her way towards the back door. Once outside, she trudged through the back garden, and then headed towards the fields.

She spotted a small flock of dragonbirds in the sky. Illuminated by hanging lanterns, their hooked beaks and feathered wings sliced through the air, aiding their delicate, scaled bodies in flight. She made a mental note to draw them after training if she felt calm enough.

These dragonbirds had different markings to the ones that came out during the day; Ray rarely saw those due to her sun sensitivity.

She approached the arena with regret. It too was abundantly illuminated with an array of hanging lanterns. As she planned which weapons to use, she anticipated defaulting to the twin blades – one in each hand. Every time she used them, they felt like an extension of herself, much like her paintbrushes. Although training could be dreary, she could appreciate the excellence of her weaponry.

Tapping her now-extended claws upon the fabric of her leggings, she entered the arena. Her mind whirled with a combination of thoughts. Part of her was looking forward to releasing some pent-up tension, but predominantly, she wanted to get the training over with.

Chapter Three

Surrounded by green fields and dashes of white paint markings to indicate proper battle positions, Ray walked further into the arena. Without her mother around, she decided to ignore the dabs of paint as she approached the training dummies.

Some of the dummies were stuffed with hay, and others were stuffed with sand. The variations in weight served different purposes for a range of training objectives. On this occasion, Ray decided that not only did she want to practice hacking and slashing, but the art of getting behind an opponent. She focused her energy, and clapped her clawed hands three times in the direction of one of the dummies on a pole.

The dummy began to shudder, some strands of hay coming loose from it, all whilst the face on its lumpy head remained as expressionless as its potato-sack limbs. Suddenly, with a mechanical clank, the pole it was on jolted forwards.

Ray darted towards the edge of the arena, grabbing her blades and swiftly intercepting the dummy as it came charging towards her with unnatural speed. She had chosen a high difficulty level for this session. Years upon years of training had led to her honing her skills, enabling her to face harder challenges. She hacked and slashed at the dummy. As more hay came out of it, she grinned at the lacerations she'd made in the cloth.

Her opponent suddenly seemed to vanish, only to re-appear behind her. Its thick arms slammed against her back, sending her flying forwards. She landed on all fours in a crouching position, and nimbly turned around with the grace of a feline on the prowl. Facing the dummy again, with her vampiric speed and twin blades, she administered several blows to its face and its arm.

She sliced off its other arm, inwardly cheering as it landed with a thud. Shedding even more hay, the dummy jolted towards Ray again. She was too fast for it. She jumped to the side just in time to avoid a heavy impact. With a chuckle, she pivoted, charging towards her opponent and sinking her blades into where the shoulders would be on a living enemy.

She then sliced downwards, doing as much damage as possible. She wasn't ready to conclude her assault yet. Kicking the dummy to the ground, she pounced on top of it. She carved into its chest with one blade, and into its neck with the other.

With the artificial challenger defeated, Ray wiped the sweat from her brow. She stood tall and rolled her shoulders back, satisfied with her work. It was now time to carry out her usual exercises, the goal being to engage in another challenge again at the end of the training session.

Suddenly, she was distracted by a low growling noise coming from within the shadows of the arena. Before she had time to enquire, she noticed a set of piercing silver eyes glaring at her. A dark shape barrelled straight towards her and rapidly began clawing at her arms. Crying out in surprise, Ray shoved her new attacker away and jumped to the side, panting and trying to catch sight of their identity, but luck was not on her side.

Something slammed into her back and sent her falling to the ground. Immediately, her attacker got on top of her and shredded into her shoulder blades, leaving cruel lacerations upon them. Using all of her strength, Ray bucked. Forcing her attacker away, she rolled into a crouching position, successfully dodging another lunge.

In that moment, Ray's eyes met with her mother's. Her heart sank as she realised this must be a test. Although it had happened before, it was always unexpected. Strands of hair fell into the older woman's face as she savagely bared her fangs at Ray.

Ray's mother drew knives and went in for another lunge. A clean cut formed on Ray's cheek; although she had jerked her head back, she hadn't been fast enough to avoid contact.

Using the acrobatics and agility she had been working on, Ray skilfully lured her mother away from the centre of the arena. She deftly sliced at her mother's arms, being careful not to cut through them. Despite their differences, she had no desire to cause her mother true harm.

Equally matched in strength and speed, the two exchanged blows, until eventually, they were circling one another like lions fighting over a meal. Suddenly, Ray lunged forward and lashed out with a series of quick strikes. Finally bringing her mother down, she crouched at the side of her, holding her twin blades in an X-formation over her neck.

The older vampire glared up at Ray and clicked her fangs.

"You managed to get me this time, Raylene. Your victories are increasing."

The slight hint of approval in her mother's tone made Ray's heart flutter a little as she rolled off and away to stand and straighten up. Her mother stayed on the ground for a minute or so.

Eventually, the older vampire stood up, approaching Ray with a half-hearted smile.

"I suppose my skills in the arena aren't to be considered rubbish?" Ray asked bitterly.

"I just want you to focus on the things that matter, Raylene," her mother replied, a slight hint of guilt in her tone. "You've got so much potential. I don't know why you waste time on pointless things like painting."

"It's not pointless to me," Ray insisted, her words laced with exasperation. "What if I went out and killed a demon – and brought the head back to prove it? Would you get off my case then?"

Ray didn't really want to kill a demon. She was just hurt, and at a loss as to how she could make her mother understand.

"Oh, Raylene," her mother said delightedly. "You are finally ready to go out and make this family proud? Yes, of course I will leave you alone to waste time on your art if you can prove to me that you *can* hunt a demon. After all this time, I think you are ready. I'm so happy to hear that you're willing to accept what you truly are."

Although Ray wasn't completely on board with what her mother wanted, she accepted the rare words of enthusiasm with a nod. Her stomach churned as she wiped her blades clean and let out a sigh.

"I'll leave tomorrow."

With that, the training session was over. Ray dismissed herself and made her way back to the house. When she got there, she wasn't in the mood to speak to anyone else. When her father and brother attempted to strike up conversation, she shrugged them off and told them she wanted to be left alone.

Despite the agreement she had reached with her mother, Ray wasn't feeling overjoyed by any means. Her shoulders slumped as she approached her bed, exhaustion settling in and causing her to yawn. As the sight of the ruined painting caught her eye, she decided she didn't have the energy to bother doing anything with it.

She tucked herself into bed, pulling the soft silken sheets up to her chin and closing her eyes. Her head swam with a thousand questions. She didn't even know how to *find* a demon!

If me slaying a demon doesn't make them happy, then I don't know what will.

Exhausted, she drifted off to sleep. Her dreams consisted mostly of nighttime nature scenes splotched in red paint.

Chapter Four

After a restless sleep, Ray got out of bed and wearily approached the mirror. As she pulled a brush through her raven hair, she considered her options. Directly seeking out demon territory in Lar would be too dangerous for her; as a vampire, she'd be as good as dead. However, she could wander near the fringes of what was technically considered no man's land. Perhaps there, she could find a stray demon, slay them, and present the head to her family.

Deciding that the latter was her best course of action, Ray tied her hair back so that it wouldn't hinder her in battle. She then gazed around at her paintings. As she mentally bid them goodbye, she sighed heavily. Her eyes shifted to the ruined one, and, after considering it for a moment, she finally decided to place it gently in her 'in progress' drawer instead of throwing it in the bin. She couldn't quite explain why she didn't just throw it out, but there was a glimmer of hope that maybe one day, the painting could be fixed.

Finally, Ray put on thin black leather clothes and left her room, descending the stairs. There, she met the eyes of Alden, who intercepted her before she could slip away unnoticed. Emitting a frustrated growl, she focused on her older brother. He was clad in his typical casual gothic attire.

"I'm busy," Ray blurted out. "I have something to prove."

"I'm aware of that," he said, sensing his sister's agitation. "I hope you know that *I'm* proud of you. I think your paintings are wonderful. I wish Mother and Father could appreciate them too."

Alden had often attempted to connect with Ray more, but his passive approach with their parents had usually resulted in her ignoring him. However, things were different on this occasion.

Ray glared at her brother. The two of them stood silently on the stairs, surrounded by walls adorned with several paintings of beautiful faraway landscapes. Despite the gloomy wallpaper and dark floorboards, the scenes in the paintings brought life to the space. Alden turned and pointed a dark nail at a piece depicting snowy mountains with giant white wolves prowling for winged antelope – common prey for predators in those environments.

"It's nice to think about other places," he said, his voice holding a hint of sadness. "It's amazing how art can inspire that."

"I would like to visit the mountains one day," Ray replied. "With our parents being so obsessed with killing demons though, exploring the world will have to stay on the backburner for now, all in favour of bloodshed."

"Yeah," Alden said with a sigh as he placed a gentle hand on his sister's shoulder. "Be careful out there, alright? You should know that you don't have to prove anything to Mother and Father."

"I know," Ray said firmly, brushing Alden's hand away and twisting her lips into a scowl. "But you know how they feel about me. It's ok for you; you're perfect – sinister, deadly, merciless. And what am I? They think I'm selfish. They view my art as worthless. I don't know much about demons, but it wouldn't hurt to prove myself. Besides, I wouldn't want there to be another war."

"You wouldn't be able to stop one anyway. Nobody would. With demons, it's just too…"

"Too what?!" Ray interrupted impatiently. "All I know is that in order to finally get approval from Mother and Father – and to get them off my back once and for all – I need to go out there and kill a demon."

Ray felt a familiar pang in her stomach. It was the one that always made itself known when the horrible feeling of sibling jealousy reared its ugly head. She had no doubt that her parents favoured her brother.

"You have their love, Alden," she said. "Perhaps you should stop trying to get in the way of me going out and getting some recognition!"

Realising she'd said that last part in a louder voice than she had intended to, Ray squirmed.

There were tales of Alden in battle, and of how he'd shown no mercy to the demons he'd destroyed. Time and time again, their parents had praised him for it.

Although Alden could see that Ray was reaching her boiling point, instead of lashing out in anger, he sadly stared at her for a moment before looking away.

"I don't really want recognition," he said softly. "I envy you, Ray. Your talents go far beyond your ability to fight. I wish Mother and Father would get off your back. The hatred for demons goes back further than anyone can remember. I don't wholeheartedly agree with it; I just accept that I have to fight for the same reason you're going out there now – to keep Mother and Father off *my* back. *I* might do it, but it doesn't mean *you* have to."

"I'm tired of them looking at me as if I'm nothing," Ray protested. "Especially Mother."

Alden looked hurt as he turned his gaze to the floor. Ray sighed. She didn't want to lecture him.

"If I promise to be careful, will that make you feel better?" she asked. "You know I have to do this, Alden. You *know*."

Alden shifted his weight from one foot to the other before straightening up.

"Yes," he said. "That does make me feel a little better. I know you're strong, and I know you're capable. Just don't lose your passion or light in pursuit of Mother and Father's approval – that's all I ask."

With that, he turned away and wandered down the hallway, probably towards his room.

The conversation had left Ray a little on edge. Although Alden had always praised her passion for art, it was rare for him to ever say anything bad against their parents. Perhaps he feared them too, but because he so rarely spoke, it was difficult to tell.

As Ray stepped out of the house, a cold breeze hit her cheek, causing her to shudder. She carried a bag over her shoulder. It contained a few bottles of blood, a medical kit, and several bags for body parts should she find herself needing to dismember a demon.

As the moon shone brightly above, she headed to the arena. Due to her being a nocturnal predator, her eyes adapted well to the dark, but the extra bit of light was always welcome. The sky was free of any cloud cover, allowing the stars to twinkle uncompromised.

Walking over a few leaves, which crunched beneath her boots, she realised that the colder season was approaching. Even then, her parents would still expect her to train.

The hatred never stops...

She sighed, already longing for her paintbrush as she entered the arena and approached the weaponry cabinet. Spotting her twin blades, she took them out and secured them to the sheath on her belt. Ready to go, she turned and nearly jumped out of her skin when she found her mother standing right beside her.

"You need to be more aware of your surroundings if you want to take down a demon," the older woman said, her tone dripping with disapproval.

Despite her words, Ray's mother was smiling. Both vampires were slightly embarrassed, but they chose to ignore the awkwardness.

"It's good that you're finally taking some

initiative, Raylene. You will make this family proud. I know I go on about your hobby, but in the end, *this* is what matters. When you slaughter one of our enemies, you will truly know what it means to be a vampire."

Rather than return her mother's smile, Ray pushed past her. She didn't appreciate her comments.

"I know I'll only matter to you when I return carrying a demon's head," she said bitterly.

She didn't bother to turn around to see the shocked expression on her mother's face. Instead, Ray practically melted into the shadows as she headed towards what she cautiously suspected was her destiny.

Chapter Five

As soon as she was clear of her family's territory, Ray felt a weight lift from her shoulders. Moonbeams danced upon her leather-clad figure as she walked along. Taking a deep breath, she revelled in the crisp air. It felt wonderful against her skin.

Her tired expression eased just a little, and a smile played on her lips. Passing by tall trees with dark trunks, she noticed the leaves already changing colour in anticipation of the winter months. Crunching over a few that had fallen to the ground, she bent down and picked one up, examining its veins and how they paired with the various jagged edges.

"Nature is the most beautiful art of all," she mused to no one in particular. "I wish I could do more to capture such beauty in my work."

"Hoooo!"

Startled, Ray quickly turned around. She hadn't been expecting a response! Her gaze fixed on a large bird with saucer-sized, flame-like eyes that glowed mysteriously. As the bird fluffed out its jet-black feathers, it seemed even grander than before. It swivelled its rounded head, surveying the landscape, before locking eyes with Ray and calling out again.

"A raven owl," Ray said softly.

She was entirely taken by the creature's splendour. The owl's crescent-shaped claws clutched the branch it stood upon as it observed her with mild curiosity. Wracking her brain, Ray tried to recall why the owl's eyes glowed like that, as it would surely give it away to its prey. She thought back to some of the nature books she had read, many of which had provided extensive detail on the creatures of Lar.

"Oh," she said with a smile. "Your eyes are like that to attract mates, aren't they?"

The owl, of course, didn't answer. Instead, it clicked its beak and froze, as if stunned by something. After a few moments, it swiftly flew away, leaving its patch of tree entirely engulfed in darkness. Ray had to blink a few times to adjust her eyes. It didn't take her long to refocus, but by the time she had, the owl had gone.

She felt a pang of disappointment; she had been enjoying the owl's presence. As she looked down at the dirt path she was wandering upon, she noticed a scattering of twigs and leaves. There was so much to see out in the quiet of nature. The peaceful stillness was too good to rush through.

Surely I don't have to go and slaughter a demon immediately?

There was so much of Lar to explore. Ray had never ventured as far before due to her parents' ridiculous rules. Now though, with her newfound freedom, she was determined to make the most of it.

She decided that it was time to transform. As she summoned the strength from within, a shimmer of crimson light surrounded her from head to toe. In a surge of power, she shed her humanoid form, assuming the shape of a small, fuzzy bat. Her fur retained the same onyx hue as her hair, and her keen ears swivelled about, capturing the sounds of the night. She delighted in the calming howl-coos of wolf-doves, but her focus honed in on the melodic squeaking of the butterbats, their enchanting song beckoning her into a realm of nocturnal wonders.

Where are they?

Taking to the sky, Ray felt the wind sweep through her fur. It didn't matter to her that she didn't possess the bedazzling powers of some of the butterbats. She hurriedly flew towards the source of the noises, performing a few spiralling loops mid-flight as she fully immersed herself in the feeling of freedom.

As the melodic squeaking grew louder, Ray spotted them: a group of butterbats flying in a dance-like manner above a clearing. Whether they were hunting or playing, she was confident that as long as they didn't feel threatened, they wouldn't be aggressive towards other bat species. She flew towards them, joining in their festivities.

In her fearless and excitable approach, Ray was welcomed by several greeting squeaks. Though she didn't understand the language, she knew the best was yet to come. Suddenly, the sky became illuminated by a dazzling array of rainbow colours – they resembled the ribbons of light in the northern skies. In the darkness of the night, the butterbats shone brightly with intricate patterns, glowing like some of the fungi found in the deep caves favoured by the goblins.

Ray let out a squeaking laugh as the butterbats did several flips and dances around her, the kaleidoscope of colours lighting up her eyes, and more importantly, her world. She would need to paint this, for it was the happiest she had ever felt.

Sad that her time with the butterbats couldn't go on forever, Ray flew down and away from the colony. She landed at the base of a large tree, and focused on transforming back into her normal form. As the crimson light covered her small bat body, she returned to her usual appearance. Before rushing off, she had carefully concealed her bags and weapons, a decision she now appreciated. Retrieving her supplies from a nearby bush, she set off again.

As she ventured onwards, the familiar sound of leaves crunching beneath her feet diminished, indicating her exit from the woods and entry into a more barren terrain. Twisted weeds concealed small rodents that hastily scurried across her path as she walked. The moon's gleam started to become obscured by passing clouds, and with it, Ray's feelings of joy began to fade. As darkness shrouded the surroundings, the colours of Lar's landscape grew dull – a change that wasn't much of an issue for a vampire, but it certainly left the world looking less vibrant.

Reminded of her mission, Ray bit her lip. She ran her hand over the sheath where her weapons rested. Walking over a bald patch of cracked ground, she felt the rocky and uncomfortable texture beneath her feet. In the shadows, she noticed the skull of an equine-like creature staring emptily at her, adding to the overall landscape of woe. She knew it wouldn't be the only instance of death she would come across on her journey.

As she continued to walk, time seemed to stretch on. Navigating through tangles and thorns, she had to be careful not to cut herself on the dreaded plants. After fighting her way through the brambles, she finally emerged into a clearing, taking a moment to catch her breath.

No chirps or buzzes of wildlife could be heard.

The entire clearing seemed to hold its breath, as if frozen in time. Ray's eyes fell upon the scattered remains of various humanoids in all shapes and sizes. Amongst them, she noticed not only fanged skulls, but *horned* skulls.

Demons?!

Deciding that it was best to navigate with some knowledge, Ray unfolded her map. She had been walking in one general direction for a while and needed to gather her bearings. Although she wasn't used to reading maps, she traced her route from home with a dark nail, following the various lines until she recognised her current location.

This was a battlefield only a few decades ago.

Frowning, Ray gulped and looked up again. She noticed flat, rounded grey stones protruding from the earth. As she walked closer to them, it dawned on her that they were gravestones. The further she walked, the more rows of stones she passed. There were quite possibly several hundred of them. She couldn't tell for sure, but it was certainly a large expanse of graveyard.

Sensing that she must be in a demon-owned

graveyard, Ray crouched down before one of the stones. Upon it, was the symbol of a skull with horns, along with the heartfelt message: *'Rest in peace. The battle took you from your family far too soon, Mother. May you find happiness in paradise.'*

Ray had never heard of demons being welcome in paradise. Throughout her life, she had been told that they were soulless and embodiments of evil. However, as she stood in the graveyard, she could almost feel the weight of sorrow hanging in the air. Curious, she moved on to another gravestone, and to her surprise, it marked the resting place of a vampire. The inscription read: *'You were slain in a pointless war. Rest well. Thank you for your sacrifice.'*

Huh? What's going on? The vampires and demons of Lar…

Ray didn't have chance to indulge in her thoughts any further, for out of nowhere, a loud, snarling screech echoed through the air.

From the shadows, burst forward a creature she'd never seen before. Its legs were much longer than its arms – which were not particularly short. It had greyish feet with four toes and large crescent claws of a darker hue. Crimson-red fur covered its legs and continued up to its midsection. Wearing black shorts, the creature had no other items of clothing upon its body.

Its torso was bare, resembling that of a humanoid male with well-defined musculature. Its arms were also humanoid-like, each with five fingers and fairly long claws matching the charcoal colour of those on its feet. Sharp blades ran down its spine, visible to Ray as the creature bolted towards her on all fours. A long, whip-like tail with a blade at the end lashed viciously behind it.

Immediately, Ray drew her blades, holding them in an X-formation as the creature charged at them. Now that it was up close, she noticed that despite its hunched back, her opponent matched her in height. She also managed to identify it as a species of demon known to vampires as 'devils'.

Its humanoid face – a darker red than the fur on its legs – formed into a scowl, revealing a maw full of serrated fangs. The tiny black horns on its forehead looked as sharp as Ray's blades. The creature stared her down with pitch-black eyes. In that moment, she also noticed its head of curly hair. The same colour as its fur, the mid-length locks spilled slightly over the creature's pointed ears.

Suddenly, the demon vanished for a brief moment before reappearing at Ray's side. It swiftly raked its claws along the leather of her clothing, piercing her flesh. Ray couldn't help but scream in anger and pain. She whirled around, now facing the demon directly, and lunged forward, stabbing with her blades. The steel met flesh as the demon cried out in agony, emitting a screech that caused Ray to wince.

The demon vanished again, only to reappear by Ray's other side as it sank its jaws into her leg. It tore out a small chunk of flesh, quickly chewing and swallowing it. Ray felt sick, but also fuelled in her desire for revenge. She retaliated by slicing a blade downwards into the demon, creating a deep laceration on its shoulder that caused another cry of pain.

Changing strategy, she lunged towards the demon, leveraging her sudden advantage to knock it down. She momentarily allowed her blades to clatter onto the dirt as she grabbed the creature by the shoulders. Extending her fangs, she sunk them into its flesh, tasting the unfamiliar smoky flavour of its blood. After just a few sips, the demon had vanished, and already Ray could feel its weight on her back.

Blood began to pour down her sides as claws tore into her flesh, forcing a furious snarl to escape her lips. Against the demon's dedicated hooks, she bucked and thrashed, eventually freeing herself. She urgently lunged for her blades. With them in her hands, she administered a series of violent swipes. Several blows landed upon her opponent's flesh, forcing them to whimper as their crimson blood splattered all over her.

Baring their teeth, the two enemies circled each other. Both were covered in open wounds.

Suddenly, the demon took several steps back and fell to its knees. Ray allowed her shoulders to slump, feeling the exhaustion from the intense battle. Overall, the two rivals were evenly matched. The vampire knew that any further attempts to thrust at the demon would result in a fierce defence. At best, she'd suffer more damage, and in the worst-case scenario, it could prove fatal.

Staring at the demon, she spat out some blood, still panting from their fight. She considered the possibility of playing for time to recover somewhat, and then taking the enemy down. However, to her surprise, the demon began to speak.

"Damn vampires! Go away! Can't you let me mourn for five minutes?!"

The voice that reached Ray's ears was unmistakably masculine – deep enough to be noticeable, but not overly intimidating. Nonetheless, it caught her off guard, causing her to stumble and land in a sitting position. She instinctively placed her blades on her lap and stared at the kneeling demon, a puzzled expression on her face as she paused for a moment to gather her thoughts.

"What?!" she exclaimed.

"That's why I'm here!" the demon said angrily. "I assume you're here to hunt me down so you can rip me to shreds, just like your kind did to my parents! If you insist on trying to kill me, you better believe it that *you* won't make it out alive."

His expression almost remorseful, the demon lashed his tail and fixed his jet-black gaze upon Ray.

"Your parents?" she asked. "If this is a demon graveyard, then why are there vampires buried here? That's blasphemous!"

"Piss off!" said the demon. "You must be one of those vampires who enjoys killing demons for the sheer sport of it – maybe through hatred, maybe through ego. Either way, I didn't ask for this."

"I… I've never killed anyone," Ray confessed.

The demon rolled his eyes, his mouth forming into a scowl. Now that he wasn't snarling like a rabid animal, he looked rather cute instead of terrifying. Shakily, he got to his feet. Letting out a sigh, he began to inspect his arms, running his claws over the many lacerations.

"You intruded on my mother's grave," he told Ray. "I attacked you first because I'm tired of your kind desecrating it."

Feeling a pang in the pit of her stomach, Ray looked down at her nails as an awkward silence hung in the air for a moment.

"I'm sorry," she said solemnly.

The demon ran his claws through his hair as he pondered the situation. Finally, he spoke.

"Oh," he said cautiously, a hint of resignation in his voice. "Vampires usually keep fighting until I chase them off, or vice versa. Either way, I always have to fix the mess they make of the demon gravestones here."

"That's horrible," Ray said, briefly closing her eyes in regret.

"Yeah," the demon agreed. "I'm Charl, by the way."

"I'm Ray. Well, Raylene, but I prefer to be called Ray," she said, giving a half-hearted smile. "I'm sorry for what you have to deal with. It's not right."

"Well, it's nice to meet someone who feels that way," Charl replied, looking up towards the sky.

Am I really conversing with a demon?! I was supposed to kill him to prove myself to my family once and for all. What have I done?!

Chapter Six

"I was taught to hate your kind," Ray explained. "I was told that you all murdered our extended family, and that you have no souls."

The vampire and the demon sat next to each other companionably, gazing up at the moon. As the clouds shifted, an ethereal light fell upon the graveyard, illuminating some of the scattered bones. The sight sent shivers down Ray's spine.

Unfazed, Charl took a cloth from his bag and wiped the blood off his body. Seeing this, Ray shuffled over to her bag. Giving the demon a reassuring smile, she pulled out the medical kit.

"Here," she said as she passed it to him. "You look pretty beaten-up from the blades I used on you."

Charl cautiously reached out and accepted Ray's

offer of the medical kit. He then took out some disinfectant wipes from it and began to properly clean his wounds.

"Thank you," he said, his tail twitching like that of a curious cat. "I must say, you're the first vampire I've ever sat down with for a full conversation. Generally, I even avoid the vampires my family are reluctantly friendly with. Apparently, the only place in Lar where demons and vampires are truly at ease with each other is in the town of Megara. My family have always told me to be wary, and that approach has never failed me. I've always trusted my instincts. Strangely though, my gut isn't saying nasty things about you."

"I wouldn't be so sure of that," Ray said. "Although I've never really had a good relationship with my family, I was hoping to prove myself to them by bringing them the head of a demon."

Noticing Charl's shocked expression, Ray immediately felt uncomfortable with her admission. She averted her gaze from him and coughed awkwardly. Charl snorted and shuffled away to create some distance between them.

"All I've ever wanted to do is paint and explore the wonders I've seen," Ray expressed. "Lar is such a vast and beautiful place. I've been longing to capture the essence of the butterbats in my art – even more so now after having experienced flying with them earlier tonight."

Charl perked up, his eyes widening as his features shifted into an expression of joy.

"Butterbats?!" he exclaimed. "You flew with the butterbats?! That's amazing! And you paint? Wow! I do too."

"Really?!" Ray asked, taken aback by Charl's enthusiastic response. "I've never met another painter before."

As she rubbed her temples and closed her eyes, the tension in her muscles began to subside a little. Opening her eyes, she spotted Charl rummaging through his bag. His energy didn't feel dangerous anymore, so she didn't question his motives. She figured that if he truly wanted to attack her with a weapon, he would have probably done so already.

From his small bag, Charl withdrew a neatly-folded piece of paper. With precise movements of his claws, he unfolded it. The paper displayed a beautiful scene of a flower-filled field. Reds and golds adorned the landscape, accompanied by delicate ivory plants carefully placed among them. The petals spread out in a mesmerising array of colours and patterns. Ray felt deeply moved by the image before her. In the scene, diurnal butterbats danced around the flowers, adding to the bright emotions that caused her soul to stir.

"Your art is beautiful, Charl. My kind can't see the fields in the day in all their glory; we're too sensitive to the sun. Does the world really look like that in full daylight? It must be wonderful."

Honoured by Ray's reaction to his art, Charl beamed, his cheerful grin widening even further.

"Thank you," he said. "I'm starting to feel happy that we've met. I carry this painting around with me because it was the last one I did before vampires murdered my mother. It's the best, most beautiful thing I have to remember her by; she loved the piece so much."

Ray hung her head. Although Charl was reluctant to pry, he couldn't help but acknowledge the vampire's defeated demeanour.

"Hey, are you ok?" he asked. "Was it something I said?"

"No, not at all," Ray answered. "I just wish my family weren't so against my desire to paint. They want me to train, to become a warrior for this big war they can't stop fantasising about. When I look at this graveyard, it makes me wonder if my parents' obsession is far more pointless than I had first assumed. My family is strongly anti-demon, and there's clearly such a big misunderstanding where they insist that your kind is just pure evil. If they knew the truth, then maybe – just maybe – they wouldn't hate me so much for wanting to focus on my art instead."

"I hope you don't take this the wrong way," Charl said nervously. "But I sense that you're better than your family."

He ran his claws through the fur on his legs, slightly perplexed and unsure of what to say next. Suddenly, an idea hit him.

"Hey! Why don't we visit Megara together?" he asked excitedly. "Because vampires make me nervous, I've always convinced myself not to go. However, it seems that we're both keen to question what we have experienced so far. I sense that we are of a similar mindset, and exploring together could be safer than going alone. You don't have to decide right away, it's just an idea. Besides, I'd love to see how you paint."

Shocked by the idea, but eager to paint, Ray watched as the demon happily rummaged through his bag. He pulled out a blank sheet of paper, a simple brush, an array of paints, and a book to use as a flat surface to lean on. Ray blinked in surprise at just how much he was carrying! Nonetheless, she nodded and gladly accepted everything he passed to her.

"Hang on a moment," she said worriedly. "What if the paint bleeds through the paper and damages the cover of the book?"

Charl laughed and momentarily removed the blank paper from the book, revealing the splotches of paint that had already dotted the cover. Ray chuckled and gave the demon a thumbs-up before getting to work.

In the centre of the page, she skilfully crafted a vampire bat with crimson eyes, its fur matching the colour of her hair. Surrounding the creature, she added butterbats with wings that glowed, just as she remembered from her flight with them. Intricate patterns adorned the night sky.

Charl watched with fascination as Ray painted life into the nocturnal scene. As soon as she finished, he gasped in delight, quickly springing to his feet and breaking into a joyful dance, overwhelmed by the development.

"It's beautiful!" he exclaimed. "Your passion and talent shines through in your work. I'm ever so sorry for having attacked you earlier, but I suppose if I hadn't, we wouldn't be talking now!"

Ray let out a laugh, nodding in agreement. She stood up and rolled her shoulders back, hearing a satisfying crack as her joints set into place.

"You can keep that painting if you like," she told Charl, her tone sweet and kind.

The demon jumped with delight, meticulously folding up the dry painting and contentedly stowing it in his bag. Then, he fixed his pitch-black gaze on Ray, his eyes now sparkling with curiosity and determination.

"Let's go to Megara," he said in a hopeful tone. "Come on, it will be fun."

Ray was hesitant at first, but after a long pause, she gave a nod.

"Ok," she said. "You'll have to lead the way."

"No problem," Charl said with a chuckle, motioning for her to follow. "Let's go!"

Chapter Seven

Before leaving the graveyard, Charl made one last visit to his mother's grave while Ray observed in silence, keeping a respectful distance. It was evident that although he felt a mixture of pain and longing, overall, he didn't want to linger on the past. Shaking his head to snap out of his reverie, he forced himself to rise to his feet and take a deep breath. He then bounced deliberately along, eagerly leading the way to the mysterious town he longed to explore.

As they walked along the winding dirt path, Ray could feel butterflies in her stomach, but Charl's pleasant company helped to put her at ease. They chatted about the best scenes to paint, with the demon pointing out the angles of the branches looming above; he enthused about how he had studied them to help bring his paintings to life.

Partway through the inspiring conversation, they noticed lights shining in the distance. They seemed to blend with the stars in a whimsical fashion, as though there was magic in the air.

The pair quickened their pace until they arrived at a cluster of buildings, where the night was alive with festivities and music. Exuberant crowds were gathered in the streets – drinking and laughing and dancing with not a care in the world.

Although the atmosphere was lively, Ray and Charl were reluctant to fully embrace it. They were exhausted from their fight and the long journey. Besides, loosening up too much after their clash wouldn't have felt right. They weren't visiting this town to party; they were there in search of answers. They knew that if they wanted to discover the truth for themselves, they would have to stay in the background to an extent. Could vampires and demons truly live in genuine harmony – one that went beyond a basic level of tolerance?

As they stuck to the shadows, they could see that Megara's skyline was a mesmerising sight. The zigzagging terracotta-tiled rooftops and glimmering light of the night market stalls cast a burning glow that could be seen from miles away. A cacophony of unfamiliar sounds mingled with the scent of herbs and spices to create a symphony of tantalising delights.

Megara bustled with demons of various shapes, sizes, and fur colours. Some stood on two legs, whilst others moved gracefully on all fours. Giant demons the size of large bears mingled with their smaller brethren. The diversity of horns – curled, straight, saw-like, and more – added to the astonishing spectacle. Even more impressive were the tails – long and short, thick and thin, they whipped through the air like coloured party streamers as some of the demons danced. It was as though everyone had come together to take part in a celebration of the night.

Of course, it wasn't just demons who occupied Megara; vampires strolled around in fanciful garb. Some wore suits, or figure-hugging dresses, whilst others had opted for looser-fitting attire. Amidst the laughter, chatter, and singing, vampires and demons interacted with ease, moving together in harmony.

Some of them were gathered at a small plaza with a grand fountain and marble benches. Here, the more daring young vampires and demons had chosen to engage in a game of chance, throwing coins into the fountain and daring each other to retrieve the treasures that lay on the tiles beneath the water. Although the game seemed to stretch on forever, no one seemed to mind, for the joy of the moment was just too great to pause.

Ray and Charl paid particular attention to the art and music vendors.

"One day, when I have enough gold, I'd like to buy a banjo," the demon whispered to Ray. "I bet they are hard to learn, but fun to play."

As she listened to the sound of several instruments being expertly played, Ray smiled and gave him a nod.

"That demon band over there sounds amazing," she said. "I bet with your determination, you could play like that one day."

Having witnessed Megara for themselves, the pair decided it was time to leave. They wandered back into the woods and settled on a mossy rock. Ray let out a sigh, feeling out of breath, and hungry.

"I'll have to head home soon," she said. "Even though I'll be returning empty-handed, I feel all the better for it. In fact, I'd love to visit Megara again when I'm not so tired. Getting a brief glimpse of it was fantastic, but I can only imagine how amazing it would be to fully participate in their way of life."

"I agree," said Charl, trying to stifle an exhausted yawn. "If you promise not to send your bloodthirsty family after me, I can give you the address of my messenger box. I'm confident that you wouldn't do anything to cause me harm. I trust you."

"Thank you for trusting me. You're right," Ray said firmly. "You've taught me a lot tonight, Charl. I shouldn't have allowed myself to become so obsessed with gaining my family's approval, when, in reality, it will probably never happen. Besides, I would be foolish to ignore what I now know about the world. I just hope that when I tell my family what I've learnt, they'll understand."

A pang of guilt fluttered in Ray's stomach as she thought of Alden. He had told her that she didn't need to go against her gut feeling in a desperate attempt to appease their parents.

"Be careful, Ray," Charl said, his voice laced with concern. "Considering your family's obsession with battle and being at war against demons, their reaction to what you tell them might not be pleasant. I don't want you to get in trouble because of me."

The demon reached into his bag and pulled out a sheet of paper and a pencil. With a few swift strokes, he scrawled the address of his messenger box. Then, he stood up and bowed gracefully to Ray. She too got to her feet and respectfully bowed in kind.

"I agree that my family might not take the news very well," she said. "But I won't make any progress if I don't try. Meeting you has shown me that demons are far from soulless creatures, and that beings like you can become true friends."

"Friends?" Charl asked, awestruck. "You think of me as a friend?"

His delighted smile broadened as Ray gave a resolute nod. They exchanged a warm hug, and then, with a mixture of emotions, Ray stepped away, hopeful that she could gather the strength to face her family.

"I bid you farewell for now, Charl. You've changed my outlook, and now it's my mission to change theirs. Everything they think they know is wrong – and it's about time they saw that."

As Ray turned to begin her journey back home, her stomach growled, reminding her of how hungry she was. She reached into her bag for a bottle of blood, knowing that it wouldn't be nearly enough.

"Good luck, Ray," Charl called after her. "I hope you're successful. And thank you for being so kind."

As the cheerful demon bounded off into the shadows, Ray felt her resolve strengthen.

I hope they'll listen to me this time. Surely they will?

Chapter Eight

Ray wandered through the woods on her way back home. As she noticed the early morning sunrays peeking over the hills, she was daunted by the thought of being caught in the light. Her sensitive skin would quickly burn under the intense beams – far more rapidly than any human's. With exhaustion creeping into every muscle, she remained tense as she navigated the unforgiving terrain.

Anticipating a journey of a few hours to reach home, she felt a sense of relief when she came across a cave after walking a bit further. The cave had an earthy scent, which wasn't unpleasant. The rocky interior was adorned with stalagmites and stalactites that protruded like teeth. Having enjoyed cave explorations in the past, Ray wasn't deterred by the sight. She only wished she had more energy to spare for a thorough investigation.

She positioned herself behind a rock for cover, and then put her bag on the ground. Shimmering and shifting into her bat form, she flew up and comfortably settled in an upside-down position, using her wings to cover her face.

The melodic chorus of morning birds gradually filled the air. The songs were a familiar lullaby to Ray; they often accompanied her bedtime routine back home. Amidst this soothing reminder, however, she couldn't deny the whirlwind of emotions that dwelled within.

Taking several deep breaths and enjoying the fresh scent of the cave's dew, she drifted off to sleep.

***

Night had fallen once more, casting a reddish tinge across the sky. Ray was making her way back home, a slight unease raising the hairs on the back of her neck. The faint scent of smoke, its source unknown, triggered a nervous twist in her stomach. She followed a seemingly endless path, until a weighty silence enveloped her surroundings.

Moistening her lips, she gulped as she neared

the imposing house that was home to her family. The three-story structure appeared oddly distorted in its proportions, an air of hostility clinging to it. Much like the sky, the moon above held a reddish hue, its glow casting an almost sinister touch upon the land.

As she approached the house, Ray noticed its dry paintwork slowly peeling from the outer walls. The building appeared to tremble occasionally, prompting her to inhale sharply. The atmosphere felt oppressive, as if the air had thickened, burdening her movements. Simultaneously, the scent of smoke grew more intense.

Upon reaching the elegantly-carved front door, Ray's intuition stirred, warning her against opening it. Another distinctive scent was apparent amongst the one of smoke: the unmistakable odour of blood.

Despite her resistance, her fingers involuntarily gripped the handle as she pushed the door open. The sight before her forced a mournful wail from her lips. Alden's lifeless body lay sprawled in front of her. His form was contorted, bones protruding through torn flesh. His insides were strewn about, and the walls and floor of the house were drenched in blood. The gruesome scene caused Ray to retch.

Her eyes fell upon the floor ahead to witness the lone head of her father, the expression on his face one of agony. The pool of blood surrounding him must have poured from his neck; his body was nowhere to be seen.

A tortured scream rang through the air. It was Ray's mother, whose arms had been torn off. Her entire torso was split open, spilling out blood and guts as she stumbled into the hallway.

"THE DEMONS DID THIS!" she screamed. "CAN'T YOU SEE?! YOU LET ONE GO! YOU LET ONE GO!"

Unable to tear her gaze away from the heart-wrenching sight, Ray stood frozen to the spot, helpless as her mother trembled and then crumpled to the ground, lifeless.

***

Letting out a startled screech, Ray plummeted down towards the ground and landed with a jarring thud, her tiny bat body gasping for air. In a dazed state, she began to shimmer as she shifted back into her vampire form. Still panting, she scanned her surroundings, wincing as her sensitive eyes caught sight of the sunlight. Although the gloomy interior of the cave didn't offer much comfort after the disturbing dream, the oppressive sun outside was far more unwelcoming.

Regaining her orientation, Ray winced at the tingling sensation on her skin, a clear warning to seek shelter from the sun before it could burn her fair complexion. She hurried deeper into the cave, further into the safety of the shadows, and pressed her fingers against her temples. As she replayed the disturbing dream in her mind, her cheeks were soon dampened by warm tears. Swiftly, she brushed them away.

I'm being unreasonable. It was a horrible dream, but rationally, I know that nothing like that would happen in reality.

She calmed her racing mind by thinking about Charl. He was a kind demon, and he had revealed the truth to her. The unsettling dream had to be merely a concoction of twisted falsehoods.

Feeling her rapid heartbeat thumping against her chest, Ray couldn't ignore her lingering exhaustion. Although reflecting on the adventures she'd had helped to calm her a little, the weight of her worries remained palpable. A sinking realisation gripped her as she acknowledged her fear of telling her family about her experience.

No! I can't let myself succumb to this fear! My family will understand. They have to! I saw the truth right before my eyes!

With that, Ray looked up at the rough cave ceiling and let out a sigh. She knew she would need to embrace its refuge for the remaining hours of daylight. Hoping to get some essential rest, and wishing for better dreams, though reluctant, she transformed back into a bat and settled upside-down on a stalactite, urging herself to relax.

I have to believe that everything will be ok.

As her surroundings began to fade, a new scene started to unfold in her mind.

***

Under the bright moonlight, Ray walked through an almost-serene mist. Blurry-but-vibrant colours danced throughout the hazy whiteness as butterbats gracefully weaved through the low-hanging clouds. Ray smiled from within as a comforting warmth surrounded her. All her worries seemed to vanish as she journeyed back home, her sense of direction unaffected by the unusual weather.

Sensing a presence beside her, she turned her head to find a crimson-skinned demon with small horns and a flickering tail. It was Charl, his gentle smile lighting up his face.

"What are you doing here?" she asked.

"I'm going to help you talk to your family," he replied.

With Charl by her side, Ray emerged from the woods and continued onwards to the large house in the distance. The fog cleared, and the lights flickered through the windows, providing a rather cheerful atmosphere. The vampire felt her optimism rising.

"I've brought my painting with me. I'm going to show it to them," Charl enthused. "I feel it will

help to get the message across that they should be more open-minded. I'm certain that everything will be ok."

Placing her trust in Charl, Ray decided to believe him. As they neared the front door and her hand reached out to open it, a fleeting memory of the previous dream crossed her mind, prompting a sudden gasp. In that moment, Charl placed a soothing hand on her arm. She turned her head to meet the gaze of her demon companion.

"I think their prejudice is poisoning your mind," he assured. "You've witnessed the truth for yourself. Just explain it all to them and give them the chance to understand – I'm sure they will."

With a nod, Ray squared her shoulders and pushed the door open. Stepping into the hallway, she held her breath as her gaze swept the area, her eyes narrowing against the sudden onslaught of bright light. Everything appeared to be in order. The cushions seemed as though they had hardly been touched. Neat stacks of books on strategy and combat graced the side tables. Yet, the most important sight was Alden. Sat in a chair with a book in his lap, his eyes widened in surprise when he spotted Ray and Charl.

"What's going on here?" Alden demanded.

Ray noticed that whilst her brother's tone wasn't an angry one, it certainly wasn't a welcoming one either. In response, she broke the news to him quickly. She told him about the graveyard battle, and about the wonderful rapport she'd established with the demon beside her, and about the incredible town they had visited.

The best Alden could do at first was to cautiously shake Charl's hand. However, upon being shown the demon's artwork, his reluctance gradually eased.

"Perhaps things can be worked out between vampires and demons," Alden finally said. "We'll still have to see how Mother and Father take it, but if their outlook can be changed, it would probably be better for everyone."

***

Ray abruptly awoke, sneezing repeatedly as the cave's dust tickled her acute senses. Still in her bat form, she felt a pang of disappointment that the more pleasant dream had been cut short. She speculated that if it had continued, the next phase might have portrayed her parents finally embracing the truth about demons, and putting an end to their unfounded hostility.

A torrent of conflicting emotions surged through Ray's mind. Performing a controlled landing – softly on the ground – she shifted back into her vampire form. Quickly grabbing her bag and slinging it over her shoulder, she peered outside the cave. It was raining heavily. A distant rumble of thunder echoed from afar.

I hope Mother and Father respond positively to what I have to tell them.

Running her nails through her silky hair and taking a deep breath, Ray readied herself to step out of the cave. Although there was moonlight peeking through the gaps in the clouds, the atmosphere was darker than usual.

With a heavy heart full of cautious hope, it was finally time for her to head home and confront her family about what she had experienced. Would either dream come true, or had they both been mere manifestations of her wishes and fears?

Chapter Nine

The sky cleared up, revealing the moon hanging above. It was a night like any other, and despite having bid farewell to Charl earlier, Ray didn't feel alone. She was confident he would be thinking of her and would be there in spirit.

As she walked through the woods, the creaking and whispers of the trees didn't unsettle her. She understood that her journey would be relatively easy compared to the challenge she was about to face in discussing a difficult topic with her family. Although her second dream had boosted her morale, she accepted it as just that: a dream.

The wind tousled her raven hair as she neared the house. At the front door, she paused for a moment. As she clasped the handle, her mind flooded with the dreams she'd had in the cave, sending an anxious shiver down her spine. The upcoming conversation with her family had the potential to result in one of two starkly different outcomes: a successful resolution, or a disastrous feud. Shaking her head as though to still her racing mind, Ray was determined to confront the uncertainty head-on and reach a definitive conclusion.

As she opened the door and stepped into the house, she immediately noticed the absence of blood. The pristine fabric of the cosy chairs in the room looked as clean as when she'd last seen them. This offered a reassuring start. Despite how vivid her unsettling dream had been, it was evident that no such nightmare had occurred in reality. Nevertheless, her stomach's persistent growling served as a reminder that she was in dire need of a good meal.

Navigating the house with tension gripping her muscles, she moved cautiously. She could hear the sound of conversation between the human servants. Upon reaching the kitchen, she felt relieved to observe that her parents were most likely elsewhere in the house.

Exchanging a smile with a compassionate human, Ray graciously invited her to provide blood. Her fangs pierced the woman's neck as she drank in a deliberate and unhurried manner. Her approach to the humans who supplied her family's sustenance was always gentle. Nobody was in service against their will. There was no need to be abrupt.

As she continued to feed, Ray shuddered at the thought of her mother. She shakily pulled away from the human, causing them to look at her with concern.

"Is everything ok?" the human woman asked softly.

"Yes, err, of course," Ray replied, turning away. "Do you know where my parents are? Have you seen Alden?"

"I saw Alden head towards the living room, if that helps," said the human.

The guidance was useful enough. As Ray continued her search of the house, the whole atmosphere felt more suffocating to her than usual. When she walked through the hallway, the painted scenes of battle caught her eye. The poignancy was impossible to ignore.

Amidst hues of onyx and crimson, the greys and

whites of metal weaponry gleamed alongside depictions of dismembered adversaries. Marked by bloodshed and brutality, the work portrayed the hostile clashes between vampires and demons. Over time, the memories of such conflicts had faded into the background for most, but for some, the bitterness remained. Ray could only surmise that her parents clung to the profound hatred – and fear – of demons.

It's ironic that I only discovered the truth whilst venturing out to kill a demon! These paintings represent something truly abhorrent. Charl's mother must have suffered dreadfully…

The thought was deeply upsetting to Ray.

After a while, she reached the living room. Amongst the darkly opulent space, was Alden. Seated in the oversized armchair where he frequently immersed himself in a good book, he seemed as though he had been anticipating his sister's arrival.

Ray raised an eyebrow, but didn't comment as Alden's eyes met hers.

"Ray! Are you ok?!" he asked, his voice tainted with concern. "I was so worried that something terrible had happened to you. I didn't want you to go away. I couldn't bear the thought of you falling prey to a demon."

Ray realised that her appearance alone was probably causing her brother to worry. She hadn't cleaned her wounds. She was still covered in dirt and deep lacerations. There was still some dried blood caked on her pale flesh and matted into her hair, which was sticking out in several places. Having been so hungry, and indeed, keen to check that everyone was ok, she hadn't given any thought to taking a shower.

Alden got up from his chair and thoughtfully approached her. One of his eyes was hidden behind his hair, but he reached up with his black nails to move it away, desperate to check on his sister's welfare.

Ray found herself uncertain about her wellbeing. The whirlwind of events had left her with little opportunity to assess herself. Nevertheless, after the unsettling dream she'd had, she was relieved to see Alden unharmed. She inhaled deeply, attempting to steady her thoughts.

"I think I'm ok," she finally replied, sounding

unconvinced of her own words.

"Did you actually kill a demon?" he asked, his doubt evident in his tone.

Ray raised her hand and rubbed her grimy fingers across her forehead. This was it, the moment that she'd been waiting for.

After a long pause, she shook her head.

"So it got away?" he asked, unable to conceal a hint of disappointment.

"No, *he* didn't," Ray said firmly, rolling her shoulders back and regaining some of her composure. "Alden, they're not like what we've been taught to expect – nothing like it, in fact. It's time to learn the truth; that goes for you, and for Mother and Father. Seriously, if you can't accept what I'm about to say, then truthfully, I know deep down that our relationship will suffer for it. Please, just hear me out. It's important. Understand?"

A fire burned within Ray's soul as she locked her gaze onto Alden, challenging him to defy her intentions. He did nothing of the sort. Instead, he meekly lowered his head. Slowly retreating, he settled into his armchair, escaping the intensity of Ray's stare. He wasn't sure what to expect of her impending words, but he sensed that they would be significant. He looked nervous as he tried to anticipate the weight of his sister's forthcoming revelation.

Ray was almost offended that Alden looked so anxious.

He's not the one who's had to go through this!

Unable to contain her emotions any longer, Ray delved into the story. She recounted her discovery of the shared burial ground for vampires and demons, providing details about her intense clash with Charl. She then revealed the true nature of the demon and disclosed their journey to Megara.

Although his expression had remained unreadable whilst he'd been listening to Ray, at the mention of Megara, Alden's eyes widened.

"What's wrong?" Ray asked warily, placing her hands on her hips and narrowing her gaze.

"As part of my training, Megara has always been described as a battleground," Alden responded. "Mother has stressed that quite often, actually. She left no room for misunderstanding, emphasising that it's far from a peaceful place."

Ray rolled her eyes, tired of all the obscurities and downright lies.

"Considering everything I've just shared with you, where do you stand now?" she asked, her urgency to have Alden on her side carefully masked.

"I've always been attentive to your words," he answered. "But I've hesitated to voice my opinions against Mother and Father, due to their unwavering beliefs and forceful approach. I should have stood up for you more. I'm sorry, Ray. I could have done more, and I'm at fault for that."

"Saying sorry doesn't change the fact that you say nothing when they treat me like crap for doing my art," Ray snapped, letting out a heaving breath. "Every time they do it, it makes me feel so small."

Ray had never previously confided in her brother about how his passive nature had left her feeling isolated within the family.

"I understand that my apology doesn't fix things," Alden concurred. "You're right. I want you to know that I do believe you. It's just that all of this is overwhelming. I've grown up with the notion that demons are terrible creatures. I've even taken the lives of a few, and..."

Seeing the disappointment on his sister's face, tears welled up in Alden's eyes and began to stream down his cheeks.

"Who's to say that those demons were anything other than innocent?" he mused, his expression shifting to a haunted one.

He buried his face in his hands, his body shaking as he sobbed. This wasn't the response Ray had been anticipating. She stood there momentarily, feeling a sense of awkwardness. However, she quickly shook off her hesitation, reminding herself that Alden had always wished for her safety. She approached him gently, and in a compassionate gesture, placed her hand on his shoulder.

"We can be the change that's needed now," she said softly. "You listened to my story, and I can tell that it has truly affected you. It's now time for me to go and talk to Mother and Father."

"They won't take it well," Alden said firmly, lifting his head from his hands. "This time though, I'll stand with you. All those times when I sat there saying nothing, you were hurting. I was wrong to let that happen. I'm here for you now."

Ray had long yearned to hear those words from Alden. They infused her with a newfound confidence and alleviated a portion of her anxiety about confronting their parents – even if only a little. A humble smile spread across her face, and as she exhaled, her body felt ever so slightly less like a coiled spring.

"Thank you, Alden," she said mercifully. "Where are Mother and Father?"

"They're in the dining room," he replied, studying his sister with a worried frown. "Your new demon friend might be kind, but the marks from your battle with him are on display all over you. Are you sure you don't want to get cleaned up first – just to make yourself look more presentable?"

"There's no time for that," Ray said, shaking her head. "After everything that's happened, I need to talk to them *now*."

Chapter Ten

Ray found her parents in the dining room. They sat stiffly, each with an elegant glass of wine in front of them.

Standing in the midst of an uncomfortable silence, Ray was acutely aware of the tension. With the blood stains on her being so evident, it only added to the awkwardness that hung in the air. Her mother, seemingly already offended, broke the silence.

"I assume you've completed your mission?" she coaxed. "I must confess, I felt a twinge of concern when you told me your plan, but given your track record in training, I was confident in your ability to defeat a demon. I didn't expect it to be a walk in the park, but I knew you were set on proving yourself, and rightly so."

Ray suppressed the urge to roll her eyes as she

approached the table. She rested her palms on its surface, and made eye contact with her mother in a penetrating crimson glare.

"Actually, Mother, we need to talk," Ray said softly, but with determination.

"What do you mean, Raylene?" she asked irritably.

Ray didn't care that her mother's demeanour carried a sour edge. She squared her shoulders and boldly bared her fangs, still locking eyes with the family matriarch. She had grown weary of being bullied and belittled simply for embracing her true self.

Having entered the room unnoticed, Alden stood tensely behind his sister, but didn't say a word.

"What I'm trying to say, is that you've got things all wrong," Ray insisted. "Demons don't have to be our enemies. I discovered so much on my journey and…"

"This is outrageous," her mother said. "How could you…"

Ray let out a loud snarl, causing everyone in the

room to freeze. She hissed, her eyes flashing. As she angrily ran her tongue over her lips, the foreboding energy in the room was overwhelming – so thick that it could practically be cut with a knife. Never before had she retaliated like that against her mother.

"Allow me to speak," Ray insisted, her tone weighted with unwavering certainty. "During my journey, I engaged in combat with a demon named Charl. When we realised that we were equally matched in strength, his words gave me pause, which led to a conversation between us. It became apparent that our battle had taken place in a graveyard that serves as a resting place for both demons and vampires. Charl was there to visit his mother's grave, seeking no conflict. Remarkably, he shares a passion for painting, just like me."

Ray's father sat silently, gulping and staring down at his nails. His shoulders slumped as he tried to process everything Ray had just said. Although he looked relieved to see his daughter back from her travels, he seemed shocked and uncomfortable with the details. Meanwhile, Ray's mother wore an expression of outrage. She snarled before speaking.

"You had a chance to kill a demon, and you *let him go?!*"

She stood up and moved hastily towards Ray.

Despite her mother's face being only inches away from her own, Ray didn't recoil. Instead, she braced herself to confront her adversary directly, baring her fangs as a low growl emanated from her chest.

In a desperate attempt to halt the escalating conflict, Alden stepped in between the two women. However, before he could fully intervene, his mother forcefully backhanded him, propelling him into the wall with alarming strength. The impact jarred his back and left him winded, much to Ray's horrified astonishment.

"How dare you?!" Ray snapped at her mother. "He didn't deserve that!"

The room fell into a strained stillness as their mother's hand arched above Ray, her nails elongating into menacing claws. Ray stood her ground, fixated on the scarred hand that bore evidence of years of combat. Although everything felt as though it was happening in slow motion, in reality, her mother's furious blow landed on her cheek within a mere second.

Immediately, a red mark quickly began to emerge on Ray's face. As well as superficial damage, her mother's claws had marred her skin with deep lacerations.

As Ray stumbled back in shock, a whimper escaping her throat, her father rose from his seat at the table with a growl.

"That's enough!" he commanded.

Regrettably, it was too late. Ray, without looking back, forcefully pushed past her mother and sprinted out of the dining room. She raced up the stairs to her bedroom, and swiftly slammed the door shut, locking it for good measure. Overwhelmed, she buried her face in her hands and let out a stream of choked sobs.

She hadn't anticipated things unfolding in this manner. Both dreams had been proven untrue. Whilst she was relieved her family hadn't been torn apart by demons, the more positive dream had turned out to be overly idealistic. Although she had anticipated some resistance from her mother, the level of volatility and violence had caught her off guard.

Ray's tears mingled with her blood, bringing her attention to the depth of the cuts on her cheek. After a moment's pause, she headed to her bathroom, seeking to examine the wounds. A knock sounded on the bedroom door, but in wanting solitude, she chose to ignore it. As she traced her fingertip along her cheek, she came to the realisation of just how much force her mother had used.

Another knock resonated against her bedroom door, eliciting a frustrated hiss from her lips. Though her anger brimmed, she resisted the urge to lash out and shatter the mirror. Recognising that ignoring the visitor wouldn't grant her the peace she craved, she eventually relented, swinging the door open with a scowl etched on her face. It was Alden. His crimson eyes darted to the side at intervals, as if checking over his shoulder.

"What do you want?" Ray snapped venomously. "Can't you see I want to be alone?"

"I'm sorry," he said softly. "Ray, Father is having a conversation with Mother. Just like you and I, he also believes that she overreacted. She isn't changing her stance, but I could see a glint of guilt in her eyes."

"I doubt that she feels any guilt," Ray said with a nasty snarl. "If she did, she would agree that she was out of order."

Ray attempted to shut the door, but Alden blocked it with his foot, preventing it from closing. He looked at his sister quizzically, his already-uneasy posture seeming even more pronounced.

"What are you going to do now?" he asked, his voice barely above a whisper. "Mother is the head of the household, and we've angered her."

"I don't know," Ray answered honestly.

"Look," said Alden. "I want to show you something when you're feeling up to it. It won't help the situation, but I feel like it's something you should know about."

"Let's just get it over with," Ray said angrily. "It will just be more mud on top of the horrible pile that we're dealing with now."

Alden began to protest, but Ray stood her ground. She figured it was best to address everything while she was already upset. They walked down the hallway together, heading towards a specific door in the house. It was the one that had been locked for as long as Ray could remember.

Alden pulled a key from his pocket, unlocked the door, and entered the room, with Ray trailing behind him. As she took in her surroundings, a gasp of horror escaped her lips.

Adorning the walls were numerous taxidermied demon carcasses, each presented as a macabre trophy. Horned heads with a variety of skin tones and hair lengths were mounted on display frames, their contorted expressions frozen in agony. Other exhibits showcased severed body parts – arms and elongated, whip-like tails.

The room, which was kept in near darkness, bore an eerie resemblance to a museum of horrors. The air was heavy with the stench of death and decay, which seemed to stick to the back of Ray's throat like a bitter aftertaste.

Other corners of the room revealed aged, corroding blades; swords and knives encrusted with the dried blood of demons. Ray could almost hear the screams of the victims that had been tortured with them.

Even the walls, an ominous shade of blood red, served to enhance the room's overbearingly sinister atmosphere. It was as though they had been painted to support the glorification of sheer barbarity.

Ray's hand instinctively flew to her mouth, stifling a whimper as she tightly shut her eyes. Her brother stood quietly by, allowing her a moment to collect herself. When she eventually turned to look at him, her cheeks were glistening with tears.

"This room is about taking pride in war and cruelty," she said. "Have you always known about it? How could you have been ok with this? Why has everyone gone out of their way to keep it from me?"

Alden winced at the accusation. It was time to tell his sister the truth. There was no point in lying anymore.

"Mother and Father feared that you wouldn't understand," he confessed. "Whenever I asked Mother if she was ready to let you see everything here, she always insisted that it wasn't the right time and that you weren't ready. As for me, I've been misled and taught to believe all of this was necessary."

Ray pushed past her brother, unable to endure the room of horrors any longer. Among the displays, she had spotted a severed head that bore a striking resemblance to Charl. The sight had disturbed her more than anything else in the room.

Alden followed Ray back to her bedroom. He stood in the doorway as she turned to look at him. He had half been expecting her to slam the door in his face.

"I admire you, Ray," he said sincerely. "Unlike our parents, you have never lied to me. I have no reason to disbelieve what you've told me about that demon. You know what Mother's like; I have always kept quiet for the sake of an easy life. I don't want you to become like me – and thank goodness you haven't! I'm glad that you're not afraid to ask questions, and that you speak your truth."

A silence stretched between the two siblings.

"Thank you," Ray finally said. "That means a lot to me, honestly. I need to be left alone for a while though. Please."

"Of course," Alden humbly replied.

Respectfully turning to walk away, he paused as his sister spoke.

"I'm not sure what I'm going to do now," she said plainly. "If I'm gone when you return, you can keep the paintings that I leave behind."

Before Alden could protest, Ray closed her bedroom door. His heart clenched as he realised that perhaps it was time for him to make a few decisions of his own.

Chapter Eleven

Ray locked her bedroom door straight away after Alden had left. Hoping that everyone would leave her alone, she embraced the silence of being in her own space.

Hopefully Mother is too angry for further confrontation; I sure as hell am.

Knowing that it would be a soothing balm for her mind amidst the turmoil, Ray yearned to paint. However, a more immediate task beckoned: tending to her wounds and washing away the grime. With caution, she ventured to her bathroom. She scrutinised the stubborn dirt embedded in some of her wounds, a sigh escaping her lips as her eyes met her reflection in the mirror. The claw and bite marks from the battle with Charl would take a while to heal. Similarly, the mark from her mother's forceful strike was still vibrantly fresh.

Setting aside those thoughts, she picked up a cloth from the shelf and rinsed it in warm water. Carefully, she swept it over her wounds, cleansing away the amalgamation of mud and blood. Gazing back at her reflection in the mirror, she noticed the profound blend of sorrow and wisdom in her eyes. Her mirrored-self seemed to regard her with an anticipatory expression, as if enquiring about her next steps.

I wish I knew.

After getting changed into looser clothing for comfort, Ray sank onto her bed. She fixated on the dark ceiling, and for a time, she let her thoughts and the revelations wash over her, a torrent of negative emotions swirling within.

Despite her racing mind and the lingering unease, she couldn't ignore her need for sleep. She rationalised that even a short nap might help to clear her head. The light slumber she had managed to snatch in the cave hadn't been restful, so she closed her eyes, hoping that not another troubling dream would haunt her.

As she slept, the only thing she saw was the meeting with Charl, and the reality of the situation. Their conversation played over and over in her mind – so much so that when she woke up, she turned her head to the side, almost expecting to see him there.

After a mere couple of hours of sleep, Ray peeled herself from the bed, her eyes heavy with weariness as a wave of misery engulfed her once more. She shuffled her way to her desk, no longer in the mood to paint. Instead, she thought back to the work she'd destroyed in a fit of rage. Gently, she slid open the drawer, gingerly retrieved the ruined work, and set it down on the desk before her. As her gaze fell upon the once-beautiful scene now tarnished by red paint, a bitter irony seemed to hang in the air, prompting her to almost laugh at the symbolism of the moment.

Staying here will lead to that.

The longer she stared at the piece, the more she compared it to the other paintings on the wall. They were all unspoiled and featured pristine scenery.

Do I really want to stay here, only to be ruined like this painting? So what if I leave? There's nothing here for me. Even with Alden on my side, the future would be bleak. Mother's hatred for demons will never change. I think it's time to take matters into my own hands.

As the magnitude of her epiphany hit her, everything halted to a stop. She grabbed some paper from the desk, and, dipping a feathered pen into a pot of black ink, began to write a letter to her new friend.

Dear Charl,

You have taught me so much. I am entirely grateful for not only your wisdom, but also your kindness. Unfortunately, things haven't worked out with my family. Although my brother appreciates my point of view, I feel that my parents are not looking out for my best interests.

I don't know why some vampires continue to harbour such hatred towards demons, but thank you for showing me a better way.

It's time for me to take control of my own destiny. Thank you for teaching me that. I adored our time in Megara. I will be heading there now. Perhaps I will see you there someday.

Ray

She smiled as she read over her letter, confident that Megara was the best place to go. There, she would gather her thoughts and take control of her future. There would be other vampires there who, just like her, had been raised under the wings of ignorance. The thought of being around others who wanted to live in peace was inspiring.

She gently put her painting supplies into small containers, firmly sealing them so that they wouldn't spill out in her bag. There would be many wonderful things to paint on her travels.

She folded up the letter and addressed it to where Charl had told her he would pick up his post. She was relieved that they had exchanged the information before parting ways.

Opening the window and giving a couple of sharp whistles, she signalled for a carrier bat. Its form passed over the moon, and with immediacy, the creature landed on the windowsill, staring at her expectantly. Ray held out the letter for it, appreciating its beautiful black and red markings.

"Make sure it gets there safely," she instructed. "There's no need to hurry."

She didn't wish to upset Charl with the burden of what had happened with her parents. The letter would get to him soon enough.

The bat chirped in confirmation, snatching up the letter and flying out into the night.

Ray prepared her bag by attaching a loop of cloth to it. That way, she would be able to carry it in her bat form. Although the weight of it would make the upcoming flight more physically demanding, her confidence in doing what she believed was right far outweighed any concerns.

She decided to leave a note in her room. Short and to-the-point, it would convey everything she needed her family to know:

Crimson isn't the only colour that should adorn a canvas.

Placing the succinct message on top of the ruined painting, she anticipated that her family would easily spot it.

Feeling completely at ease, Ray morphed into her bat form, a beautiful glow surrounding her entire body. She grabbed her bag and perched on the edge of the window for a moment. As the wind blew through her fur and filled her small nose with the refreshing scent of Lar's great outdoors, she was ready for freedom. She would explore and paint, completely rejecting the pressure to harm another being.

She flew towards the moon, a dull past behind her, and a colourful future ahead.